The year is 1144 and the world's last dragon has returned. The evil Lord Manning plans to use that dragon to rule the kingdom. According to prophecy, only one person can stop him. And that one person is a 16-year-old boy.

BOOK 1: *The Last Dragon* Jacob, Orson and Lia must rescue the only egg of the world's last dragon.

BOOK 2: *A Hero's Worth* While the young dragon grows, Lia may be forced to marry Lord Manning.

BOOK 3: *Draco's Fire* The fully grown dragon helps Jacob fulfill the prophecy — and rescue his kingdom.

The **DRAGON SPEAKER** Series

The Last Dragon

C.A. RAINFIELD

LIBRARY AND ARCHIVES CANADA CATALOGUING IN PUBLICATION

Rainfield, C. A. (Cheryl A.)
   The last dragon / C.A. Rainfield.

(HIP fantasy)
(Dragon speaker ; 1)
ISBN 978-1-897039-46-5

I. Title. II. Series: HIP fantasy III. Series: Dragon speaker ; 1

PS8645.A433L38 2009   jC813'.6   C2009-903741-6

General editor: Paul Kropp
Text design: Laura Brady
Illustrations drawn by: Charlie Hnatiuk
Cover design: Robert Corrigan

3 4 5 6   20 19 18

Printed and bound in Canada

Canadä

High Interest Publishing acknowledges the financial support of the
Government of Canada through the Canada Book Fund for its
publishing activities.

CONTENTS

CHAPTER 1: The Chosen One 5

CHAPTER 2: The Prophecy 13

CHAPTER 3: Jacob's Quest 21

CHAPTER 4: The Dragon's Voice 34

CHAPTER 5: The Wounded Dragon 45

CHAPTER 6: Inside the Castle 55

CHAPTER 7: "If You're Lucky, You'll Die Quickly." . . . 66

CHAPTER 8: A Stranger in the Dungeon 75

CHAPTER 9: So Much Blood 87

CHAPTER 10: The Dragon's Egg 97

CHAPTER 11: Heroes 106

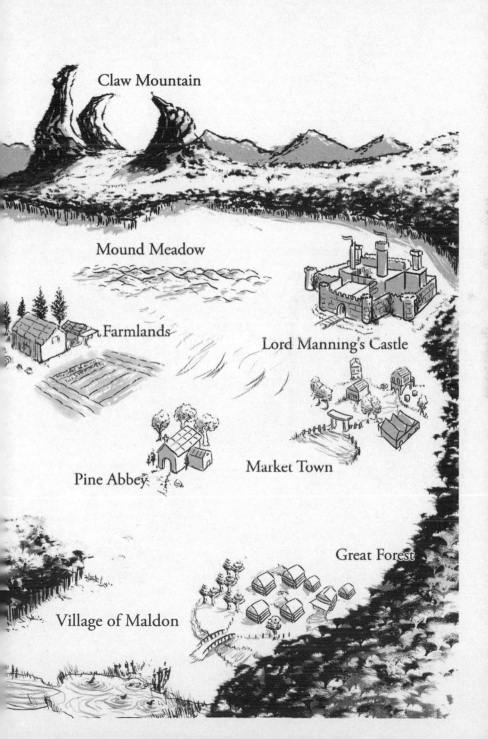

Claw Mountain

Mound Meadow

Farmlands

Lord Manning's Castle

Pine Abbey

Market Town

Great Forest

Village of Maldon

For Jean

And for anyone who's needed a book to get through something, or who knows the magic of a good story.

CHAPTER ONE | Chosen One

The birds were screaming. Their voices were so loud that Jacob thought his head might split open.

Jacob gritted his teeth. The birds were crying for help, but Jacob could do nothing. His father expected him to keep on working.

Jacob had never told his father that he could hear birds talk. He had never told anyone except his best friend, Orson. Jacob knew the other villagers would laugh. And his father would think he was crazy.

"Boy! Get a move on!" his father shouted.

At the top of the hill, Jacob tripped. Pain tore through his weak leg. He dropped the load of wood he was carrying.

"Not again!" Jacob's father cried. "You're useless!"

The words cut into Jacob like a knife. Even worse, Jacob feared that the words might be true.

Jacob ducked his head and bent to pick up the wood. His hands shook.

"No. Leave it!" his father grunted.

Jacob clenched his fists and turned away, his eyes hot.

~

Life in the village wasn't always this hard. But that was before everything had changed. When King Harold was captured and held for ransom by pirates, his kingdom fell apart. There were battles across the country. Soon it was lord against lord, town against town. At the end, Lord Manning took power. He had a wizard, Kain, who used dark magic. He had soldiers who would kill for the joy of it. And he had a plan to become king.

Ten years ago, Lord Manning's soldiers had attacked Jacob's village. The villagers had fought back, but it was hopeless. Men on foot were no match for soldiers on horses. Sharp sticks were no match for steel swords. Soon

Lord Manning's wizard killed all the male children who had magic, and set fire to Jacob's house. Jacob's mother was trapped in the burning house. His older brother died trying to rescue her. And Jacob was trapped, one leg badly burned. He had been powerless to help either of them.

Since then, there had been little joy in the kingdom. And lately things had gotten worse.

In his head, Jacob heard the birds scream again. Their voices shot through him like a hundred nails being driven into his skull. Jacob couldn't bear the pain. Somehow he had to help the birds.

Jacob limped toward the Great Forest. That's where the bird voices seemed to come from.

"Boy! Where do you think you're going?" his father yelled.

Jacob didn't answer. He kept walking toward the forest, cursing his weak leg and his slowness.

At last Jacob stumbled to the edge of the trees and stopped. His body grew cold. The forest floor was covered with birds — sparrows and finches, crows and starlings. The birds just lay there, silent and still.

All of them were dead.

Jacob stared. Blood ran from the birds' beaks. Their open eyes were glassy.

Off to one side, Jacob heard a harsh laugh. He looked

up to see Kain — Lord Manning's wizard — standing in the middle of the birds. The wizard's black cloak rose around him as if he controlled the wind. His mouth was curved in an animal grin.

Jacob shivered as Kain turned toward him. Jacob could see human teeth braided into the wizard's hair. These were trophies from men he had killed.

The wizard locked his gaze on Jacob. "Spying on me, are you, boy?"

"No . . . no, sir," Jacob whispered. He clenched his teeth.

"I ought to kill you, too, like I did the birds," Kain sneered. "But I'm rather tired of killing today."

"These birds did nothing to you!" Jacob said. Just like his brother and mother had done no harm.

Kain pointed one bony finger at Jacob. "You dare to challenge me?" Kain spat out. "You stupid peasant boy!"

Jacob stood still. He knew the wizard could kill him with a word, a single blast of magic. He waited for it, almost wanting to die.

But death did not come.

"Enough of this," Kain said, as if Jacob were no more important than an ant. "Away with you, boy." Then he pointed at Jacob. "You will not be able to speak of this to anyone." He added a word of black magic.

Jacob felt the magic strike his throat, like the butt of a sword. He felt like he was choking. He couldn't suck in enough air. He clawed at his neck, gasping, while Kain laughed.

Jacob stumbled away from the wizard as fast as he could. His head grew light and dizzy, and his chest ached.

When he was out of sight of the wizard, his breath came back in a rush. The air burned his throat and lungs. He tried to call out, but no words came. He leaned on a tree for support.

Then, over Jacob's head, a branch snapped. A crow fell from the tree and landed at his feet.

Help me, Chosen One, the crow sent a thought to Jacob. The bird's chest was rising quickly up and down. Soon this bird, too, would be dead.

How can I help you? Jacob asked, sending his thoughts to the bird. At least he didn't have to speak.

Stop the evil men, the bird replied. *They're using black magic to kill us. They are trying to call the last dragon.* The bird sent an image. In his mind, Jacob could see huge, shining scales. Then two yellow, glistening eyes, flecked with gold. Then sharp, pointed teeth with fire shooting from its mouth.

Jacob shook his head. A dragon? No one had seen a

dragon since the Dragon Wars, long before Jacob was born. Now people said there never had been any dragons. They said that dragons were only in fairy tales.

But why? Jacob asked. *I thought dragons were supposed to protect men. What's so bad about a dragon coming?*

The bird shivered in Jacob's hand. *Kain has found a way to control the last dragon.* The bird sent an image of a glowing white circle, perhaps a stone. *He will turn the dragon into a weapon to kill his enemies.*

The bird's mind voice was weak. Jacob sheltered the bird from the hot afternoon sun with his body.

Don't try to speak, Jacob sent to the bird. *You should rest.*

No, the crow sent back. *You must know this. Only you can save the dragon. Only you can stop the killing.*

Me? Jacob sat down on the damp earth and stuck out his bad leg. *Why me?*

You can talk to her. You can talk to dragons.

Jacob laughed. The idea was crazy. *No one can talk to dragons,* Jacob sent to the bird. *Besides, I thought they were all dead. Are you sure there's one still alive?*

The bird answered quickly. *Yes. You can speak to this dragon, as you speak to us. You are the Chosen One.*

"I'm not chosen for anything," Jacob said out loud. His voice had come back.

The crow's mind voice grew weaker still. *You* are *the Chosen One! All the birds know it. All the birds sing it. You must help!*

Jacob felt a flash of pain. The crow's chest stopped rising. The bird's body grew still in his hands.

Jacob struggled to his feet, then dug a shallow hole with a stick. He lowered the crow into the hole and covered the bird with earth. "Rest easy, friend," Jacob whispered.

But Jacob could not rest easy himself. He glanced back at the forest. Could the crow have been right? Could there really be one dragon still alive? And would Jacob ever hear its voice?

CHAPTER TWO | **The Prophecy**

Jacob limped back to the village, toward the black-smith's hut. His friend Orson was in the yard, swinging and thrusting with his sword.

Orson was sturdy and strong, his arms thick and his chest broad. Jacob felt like a runt when he looked at Orson. His own thin frame would never be powerful like Orson's.

Jacob stood and watched Orson practice with his sword. His friend was getting good. Maybe one day Orson would become a knight for King Harold. Jacob knew that was his friend's dream.

"Got the day off?" Jacob asked when he got close enough.

Orson grinned, then shrugged. "Pa's drunk again. And I can't work the metal by myself, can I?"

Jacob could hear some off-key singing coming from the blacksmith's hut.

"Listen, I need to talk to you about something," Jacob said.

"So talk." Orson raised his sword again and swung it in an arc.

Jacob stepped back, out of the sword's range. He opened his mouth to tell Orson about the wizard and all the dead birds. But when he tried to speak, Jacob's throat tightened. A strange noise came out instead.

Orson glanced over. "What's the matter? You swallow a fly?"

Jacob shook his head and tried again. The words still stuck in his throat. Kain's spell kept Jacob from talking about what he'd seen in the forest. Somehow Jacob would have to talk around the magic.

"There's a dragon alive, after all," Jacob said.

Orson snorted. "Who told you that?"

"Does it matter?"

Orson stopped swinging his sword. "It wasn't a bird, was it?" Orson stopped and looked at his friend. "You've been talking to the birds again, haven't you?"

"So what if I have? Just because you can't …."

"You want people to think you're crazy?" Orson jabbed with his sword again.

"I thought you believed me! Remember when the birds warned us before Lord Manning attacked?"

Orson started swinging his sword. "Maybe I believed it then. I was scared. We both were. But now — I don't know. Maybe it was just luck."

Jacob turned away from Orson. He knew no one else would believe him. That's why he'd never told anyone else. But Orson had seen it happen. Orson had heard Jacob explain what the birds were saying. And Orson was Jacob's friend. He'd never made fun of Jacob, even when the other kids mocked Jacob's leg and funny walk. And Orson had stuck up for Jacob. But that wasn't enough any more.

Jacob limped away.

"Jacob, wait!" Orson called after him.

Jacob kept walking.

Orson ran up beside him. How Jacob wished he could run like that.

"Okay, I believe you," Orson said, as he put a hand on Jacob's arm. "Why is this bird thing so important to you?"

"Swear you won't laugh?"

Orson rolled his eyes. "I swear."

"A crow told me I'm the Chosen One. He said that I can speak to dragons. He said I have to save the last dragon from Lord Manning and the wizard."

Orson stared at Jacob with wide eyes. "The bird really said that? That you can talk to dragons?"

Jacob nodded, then waited. "You still believe me?"

"It reminds me of something my pa once said. You know how he gets when he's drunk. Dragons, dragons, dragons — he won't shut up about them even though it could get him killed. But one time," Orson rubbed his jaw, "one time, it was different. I thought it was just the drink making him crazy. But maybe my pa remembers something. Maybe we can make him tell us."

Now it was Jacob's turn to roll his eyes.

Orson ignored it, tugging Jacob with him into the blacksmith's hut. The hut was growing dark; the fire flickered in the corner, almost out.

Orson's pa sat half on, half off a chair in the corner. Jacob could smell the stink of ale.

Orson's pa looked up with red eyes when they entered. "Toly, is that you?"

"No, Pa. It's Orson," Orson said. "My brother's dead. Remember?"

Jacob bowed his head. Ten years ago, Lord Manning's men had killed any male child who showed signs of magic. Both Jacob and Orson had lost their brothers. Many villagers had lost their children. Now the entire village was left with pain in their hearts.

Orson glanced at Jacob, then back at his pa. "Jacob here wanted to know about dragons."

Orson's pa wobbled, his eyes growing bright. "Ah, dragons made this land a better place, way back then. Lord Manning did wrong, killing them off." He belched. "Don't know how he did it. Dragons are fierce, you know. They used to keep a man from doing things he'd regret. They protected the weak and the poor." He snorted. "Not like now."

Jacob frowned. Was this the talk of a drunk old man or the truth? His own father wouldn't talk about the old times. He wouldn't dare — not when he could get killed for it.

Orson shrugged and turned to Jacob. "I'm sorry. I guess we're not going to get anything out of my pa. He doesn't talk about the Dragon Speaker every time."

Orson's father leaned forward. "Dragon Speaker! Do you know about him, too?" He put his finger up to his lips. "Don't tell anyone! You can get killed for repeating the prophecy."

"The prophecy? What prophecy?" Jacob asked, his heart pounding hard.

"Good boy." Orson's father winked, then laughed again. "Don't tell anyone."

"Pa, come on ...."

Orson's pa belched.

Jacob took a step forward. "The prophecy about ... the Dragon Speaker?"

Orson's father got a far-away look in his eyes. He raised his head and spoke. His voice seemed to come from somewhere deep inside him.

"When night skies blaze with Draco's fire
the darkest days shall come
until the Chosen One will rise
to speak in bird and dragon tongue."

Then the old man's head dropped. His eyes closed and he began to snore.

"Sir," Jacob said, shaking the old man's shoulder. "Is there more?"

But Orson's father slept on. The blacksmith's fire flickered and spat.

Orson dragged Jacob away from his sleeping father. Then he looked at his friend. "Maybe Jacob, just maybe, the Chosen One is *you!*"

CHAPTER THREE | Jacob's Quest

Jacob pushed away Orson's hand. The blacksmith's hut suddenly felt very small. "What are you talking about?"

"You heard my pa. The Chosen One can speak in bird and dragon tongue. *You* talk to birds. And the birds think you can talk to dragons." Orson's eyes were bright. He gripped Jacob's arm. "You're the one who's going to defeat Lord Manning! And I'm going to be right beside you, Jacob. I'm going to make him pay for what he did to our brothers."

"That's crazy!" Jacob said. "I'm not a hero. I mean, *look* at me." Jacob stuck out his frail, withered leg. "Look! How can I be a hero with this?" Long scars twisted down Jacob's leg from his knee to his ankle. The raised scars shone pink in the firelight.

Jacob hated his scarred leg. It was a constant reminder of the terror of that night ten years back. Of Kain setting fire to their hut. Of his mother screaming. Of his brother rushing to save her. But nothing could put out a wizard's fire. Jacob had seen all this, but before he could do anything a burning plank fell on his leg. If his father hadn't pulled him out of the burning hut, he would have died too. Sometimes Jacob wished he had. The way his father had looked at him ... as if he should have done something.

Jacob swallowed the bitterness that rose in his throat.

"Your leg doesn't stop you from talking to birds, does it?" Orson said. "Or dragons ... if you ever find one?"

"Since when do you believe your pa's drunken stories?"

"I thought you wanted to be seen as an equal. Stop being a coward, and go find the dragon!"

Jacob turned away, stung by his friend's words.

"Do it to get even for the death of your brother," Orson said. "You know you want to. Do it to prove that you're better than everyone thinks."

Jacob clenched his hands. Yes! He wanted to — for his brother, for his mother. And to show the villagers that he wasn't someone to pity or scorn.

"Fine! We'll search for the dragon."

Orson slapped Jacob on the shoulder. "You show them!"

"But if it turns out there isn't a dragon, we're coming back home," Jacob said.

Deep inside himself, Jacob hoped there was a dragon — a dragon that only he could hear.

But the dragons were dead. They had been dead for thirty years. Now they were only in fairy tales for little children. And Jacob didn't believe in fairy tales.

Orson walked to the corner of the hut and picked up two knapsacks, throwing one to Jacob. "Come on. Help me fill these."

Jacob limped over to the table and packed whatever Orson handed him. A loaf of bread, a hunk of cheese, three apples. A cloak to keep out the rain. A blanket to tie to his pack. A fire starter.

Orson strapped a leather scabbard to his waist and slid his sword inside, then tucked a dagger into his boot. He looked at Jacob, eying him and the swords that hung on the wall.

Jacob shook his head. "Don't bother with a sword for

me," he said bitterly. "You've seen me. I don't have the balance or the speed."

Orson took another dagger off the wall. "You can carry this," he said firmly. He fastened a strap to Jacob's good leg.

With the dagger tucked beneath the strap, Jacob felt brave — as if it made him stronger. "I should get my bow and arrows. At least I know how to use them."

Orson took down a set from the back of the door. "You can have my brother's. That should do it ... unless you want to say good-bye to your pa?"

Jacob thought of his father's anger and the shame that was always in his eyes when he looked at Jacob. "No," he said. Jacob took the bow and arrows Orson handed him, then flexed the bow. It was about the same size and weight as his own. He fastened the set to his pack.

Orson leaned over his sleeping father and shook him. The old man stirred. "Pa — Jacob and I are going away for a few days. Maybe weeks. But we'll be back."

"Wha...?"

"I'll be back," Orson said. He kissed the top of his father's head.

The old man patted Orson's hand. "You're a good boy." The old man's chin fell down to his chest, and he snored loudly.

"We're off!" Orson marched out of the hut.

Jacob followed but he almost bumped into Orson, who was just standing there.

"Uh — which way should we go?" Orson asked.

"I thought you had it all planned out."

"You know me." Orson shrugged. "Jump first, ask questions later."

Jacob thought for a few seconds before he answered. Kain had killed the birds to call the dragon. So maybe he'd left a clue. "Why don't we start with the Great Forest — where I saw the … crow." Jacob was relieved that he got the words out.

"Lead the way," Orson replied, sweeping his arm out and bowing as if Jacob were a prince.

Jacob laughed and swatted Orson's arm as his friend passed.

Together, they walked to the woods. The forest floor was empty now. All the dead birds were gone. There were only the footprints of men left on the ground.

"Now where?" Orson asked.

"I don't know. This was *your* idea!"

"Ah, but you are the Dragon Speaker. It's your mind we should trust."

Jacob crossed his arms over his chest. It seemed stupid, now, to think that there really was a dragon.

"Let's go back home before everyone knows for sure that I'm a fool."

"Jacob," Orson sighed, "come on. Believe in yourself. If you were a dragon, where would you hide?"

"As far away from the wizard and Lord Manning as possible."

"Ah ha! So we go this way," Orson said, turning away from the castle.

"But the crow said Kain had found a way to control the dragon. So maybe Kain already has the dragon."

Orson spun back around. "Then we go this way."

"But the crow wouldn't have told me to *find* the dragon if he knew where the dragon was. So — I think it's still hiding. If it actually exists."

"Then we go *this* way." Orson turned around, his back to the castle again.

"Fine." Jacob limped into the forest, walking as fast as he could. The uneven ground hurt his weak leg, but he wasn't about to let it show.

~

"This isn't working," Jacob groaned. Orson and Jacob had been walking for hours, Jacob trying to hear the dragon. But he hadn't heard anything.

Birds had started joining them early on. Now the birds flitted from branch to branch, following him. There were crows, sparrows, and finches — all interested in what he was doing. Jacob tried to be patient with their talk, but he felt angry. His head ached, his feet hurt, and the sky was getting dark. Branches kept on slapping his face, scratching his arms and neck. And the knapsack was beginning to feel heavy. Worst of all, he had the feeling that someone was following them.

"Just listen for the dragon," Orson urged him.

"I *have* been listening!" Jacob cried. "I can't hear anything."

"Well, try harder."

Jacob sighed and reached out with his mind, straining to hear….

Nothing. Again. Except the birds who kept urging him on. Maybe the birds had picked the wrong person. Maybe Jacob wasn't the person in the prophecy. "Let's stop and think about this, okay?" Jacob said as he stretched his aching leg.

"Is your leg hurting you?"

"It's fine!" Jacob snapped. "I'm just sick of looking for something we won't find. People will laugh at us even harder when we go home."

"They won't laugh at you if you find the dragon."

"I don't know *how* to find the dragon!" Jacob shouted.

"Well, you won't find it by shouting."

Jacob clenched his fists. He had let himself be talked into this. He'd let himself hope that he could be a hero. But now that seemed to be a joke.

A rabbit hopped through the brush. Jacob unslung his bow. He might as well do something useful and add to their small food supply. He sighted along the arrow and took aim. The arrow flew true. The rabbit fell to the ground, the arrow clean through its head.

Orson whistled. "You're good."

Jacob grunted. He soon shot two more rabbits, taking back his arrows each time, then tied the rabbits to his pack. When they were cooked, they'd make a fine supper.

The birds around him stopped twittering. Their voices screamed inside his mind, wailing sharply. Jacob clutched his head against the pain. He knew that hundreds of birds had just died. It had to be the wizard's doing. And Jacob couldn't do anything about it. Not here, in the forest, listening for a dragon he couldn't hear. He could hear only birds, poor doomed birds, all believing he could save them.

Behind them, a twig snapped.

Jacob jerked around in a circle, stumbling. Orson

reached for his sword. They couldn't see anyone through the brush.

Jacob limped in the direction of the sound.

No one was there, but the air smelled strongly of mint.

Jacob peered around. There was no mint growing on the ground. He'd never seen any mint in the Great Forest.

Jacob went back to a small clearing. "Nothing there," he said with a shrug. "I think we should make camp." The birds burst back into song, almost as if they were laughing.

Orson looked up at the darkening sky. "We couldn't have gone much farther tonight, anyway. Maybe we'll find the dragon tomorrow."

Jacob took off his pack, rubbing his sore shoulders. Together he and Orson gathered wood for a fire and laid out stones. Jacob felt better when he'd had some food. He even laughed at the stories Orson told.

The forest was dark, now. Jacob could barely see Orson's face across the fire.

"Things will look better in the morning," Orson said.

Jacob grunted and unrolled his blanket. He lay down, flexing his aching leg, then he stared up at the dark sky through the branches. He could see Draco — the stars that formed the shape of a dragon. They looked extra bright that night. Maybe it *was* a sign. Maybe Orson was right. Maybe they'd find the dragon tomorrow.

~

Jacob woke to a cold rain on his face. The sun hadn't come up yet. Cursing, he tumbled out of his blanket. He rolled up the damp blanket and tied it to his pack. Orson was still asleep. Jacob limped over and nudged Orson with his weak leg. "Wake up."

Orson snorted and sat up. He looked at the dark sky and groaned. "Guess we're getting an early start."

"Guess so," Jacob said sourly.

Orson rolled up his blanket and strapped on his sword. Jacob sighed and draped the wet sheepskin cloak around him, then slung his pack onto his back. The cold rain came down harder. The birds who'd been following them huddled in bushes and on tree limbs.

Jacob shivered. He dug a piece of bread out of his pack and chewed on it as they walked farther away from their village. It felt good to get away from his father — to get away from the anger and shame Jacob always saw in his eyes. Jacob could never measure up to his dead brother. But he had to try.

At noon, the rain finally stopped. It was a small mercy. Jacob slogged forward, his boots squelching in the muddy forest. The whole morning, Jacob had reached out with his mind. He kept trying to reach the dragon … if there even was one.

The mind-reaching was tiring. Sometimes Jacob thought he felt a shadow of a presence, but when he tried to focus on it, it was gone.

"What am I doing wrong?" he asked.

Orson shook his head. "Maybe the dragon's not close enough for you to hear it. Or maybe you just have to practice more. I mean, could you always hear birds?"

"Pretty much."

"Oh. So maybe you just have to wait."

Jacob glanced at Orson. Strong, friendly Orson — the one person who believed in him. "You're a good friend."

Orson grinned. "Glad you know it."

Jacob kept thinking as they walked. He *had* to find a way to hear the dragon. Maybe he'd just been going about it the wrong way. Maybe, instead of listening to voices outside himself, he should be listening *inside* himself.

Jacob stopped, set down his pack, and sat on it. "I'm going to try to reach the dragon a new way. Don't talk to me, okay?"

"Sure," Orson said. His gray eyes were serious.

Jacob closed his eyes and breathed slowly. At first all he could hear were the sounds of the forest. The squirrels scolding anyone who got too close. The wind rustling the leaves. The chipmunks running across the forest floor. Jacob shut those out, one by one, but he couldn't shut the birds' voices out of his mind. He'd managed to ignore them but never to silence them.

He focused so hard that his breath grew uneven. At last he muffled all the sounds until he had silence. Absolute silence. The world seemed to go still — as if he were deaf.

Then a roar — like the earth splitting open — tore through Jacob's head. The roar filled his brain and shook his entire body. The pain was worse than fire eating his flesh.

Jacob screamed. Red flames burst before his eyes, and then there was only blackness.

CHAPTER FOUR | The Dragon's Voice

Jacob thought that he must be dreaming. Cool hands soothed his forehead. He smelled mint in the air, fresh and bright. And then something tickled his cheek.

"Well, I think we should wake him up," Orson was saying.

Jacob opened his eyes a crack.

In front of him was a girl with deep green eyes and pale cheeks. She was looking into his face with worry in her eyes. Her golden-brown hair was covered with a scarf. A fine gold chain glittered around her neck.

Jacob struggled to sit up. His skull hurt like it had been split open. He felt sick — so sick he wondered if he'd vomit. *Please, not in front of this girl,* he told himself.

The girl pushed him gently back down. "You're in no shape to get up yet," she said. "And I'm not finished with you."

Finished with him? Jacob wondered. *What did that mean?*

Jacob tried to push the girl's hands away, but he was as weak as a bird just out of its shell. He opened his eyes wide. The girl and the forest swam in front of him.

"Rest," the girl ordered.

And sleep took him as if he were slipping into water.

When Jacob opened his eyes again, the sun was higher in the sky, and the horrible pain in his head was gone.

"So, you're finally awake," a girl's voice said.

Jacob sat up suddenly. Jacob could see a girl about his age crouched over the fire pit. Jacob's stomach growled loudly.

The girl laughed. "And hungry, too."

"Who are you?" he asked, blinking. "Where's Orson?"

"Oh, and so polite. Not so much as a thank you for mending your head . . . Dragon Speaker." She said the last words slowly, carefully.

Jacob staggered to his feet, his heart clenching in his chest. "What? No, you've got it all wrong...."

"Really?" The girl looked at him. She crouched down, waiting.

Jacob had to be careful. The girl could be a spy; she could report him to Lord Manning. Jacob studied her carefully. Her skin was pale, her mouth firm, and her eyes danced with laughter. Jacob's heart wanted to trust her, but his mind told him not to.

He'd never seen this girl before — not in the village, and not up near the castle. "You must not be from around here," Jacob said. "Lord Manning has forbidden anyone to talk about dragons."

"But he's not here right now, is he?" the girl said.

"The penalty for even using the word is death."

The girl shrugged. "I won't tell him if you won't ... Dragon Speaker."

Why was she so light-hearted? Jacob wondered. She must be hiding something; he was sure of it. Best to play dumb. "Why would you even think I am a — what did you call it, a Dragon Speaker?"

"I saw you in a vision." The girl said it simply. It was as if a vision was something that happened all the time.

The bushes rustled behind him. Jacob spun around, wondering if it was a trap.

But it was just Orson. Jacob's friend stepped into the clearing, four dead rabbits slung over his shoulder.

"Ah, the sleeping Dragon Speaker finally wakes up," Orson said. "I didn't think one rabbit would feed us all."

"Good," the girl said, standing. "He needs food and rest."

"I don't need rest! I'm fine," Jacob said.

"You want to faint again? You'll eat and rest," the girl ordered. "You have important work to do. You must be ready."

"I see you've met our mystery girl," Orson said, grinning. "She wouldn't tell me her name."

The girl tightened her lips. "It's Lia."

Orson threw the rabbits to the ground and pulled out his dagger. He pinched the skin at each rabbit's belly, and cut a hole in the skin. He cut all the way around the rabbit's belly, then pulled each half apart, stripping off the skin. He gutted each rabbit in turn, then wiped his bloody dagger on the moss. Then he thrust a stick through the rabbits and placed them over the fire.

After a few minutes, Lia took off the rabbit meat that had been cooking on the spit. She cut a huge hunk off and set it on a square of cloth. She carried it over to Jacob and set the meat before him. "Eat, Dragon Speaker."

Jacob shook his head. "I'm not the. . . ."

"You can trust me. I won't tell anyone what you can do," Lia said.

"I can't do anything. . . ." Jacob began but then stopped. He remembered now. He had heard the dragon; he knew he had. Jacob wanted to tell Orson, but he couldn't say much without Lia overhearing.

"You fainted," Lia said, still standing in front of him. "The more emotion a dragon feels, the more it affects a dragon speaker. It is very hard for an untrained person. You will need to eat before you try again."

The smell of cooked rabbit was impossible to resist. Jacob bit into it. It tasted even better than it smelled.

Jacob noticed the leaf and star tattoo on her hand — the mark of a healer. She must have shown her talent early. But that didn't explain why she was so sure that he was a dragon speaker — more sure than Jacob himself.

Lia smiled at him, her green eyes dancing with light. Jacob smiled back before he could stop himself. Was it really so bad if she knew? She didn't seem dangerous. But maybe that was all part of a plan to trap him.

"Why are you here?" Jacob asked.

Orson grabbed some meat off the spit, and sat down next to Jacob. "Yeah, Lia. Why are you here?"

Jacob and Orson both stared at the girl, waiting for an answer.

Lia looked back at them. "My family have been dragon healers for generations. After the Dark Times, after the dragons were killed, we passed down the knowledge in secret. My family knew the dragons would come back."

Jacob rubbed his jaw. Until a few days ago, he hadn't known there were any dragons still alive. Even now, he wasn't sure. If this girl really knew how to heal dragons, maybe she could help. "So — do you think there are any dragons left?"

"I know there are," Lia said. "I dreamed of a dragon. There's *one* still alive, for sure."

Jacob hesitated. "Do you know where the dragon is?" Why did the girl make him so tongue tied? And why did she smell so good? Mint — she smelled like mint. None of the village girls smelled like that.

Then Jacob had another thought. "Hey, you're the one who's been following us, aren't you?"

The girl smiled. "I knew I had to find you. I saw it in my dreams. But I wasn't sure you were a true dragon speaker until you fainted."

Orson laughed loudly. Jacob glared at him.

The girl smiled wider. "And no, I don't know where the dragon is. Do you?" She stood there with her hands on her hips, watching him.

Jacob's cheeks grew hot. "No!" He bit into some

meat, swallowing so quickly he almost choked.

Lia nodded. "I'm sure you'll find the dragon." She walked back to the other side of the fire and sat down with her own hunk of rabbit meat.

That was better. He almost felt like he couldn't think when the girl was close. Jacob ate steadily until he finished his meat. He wiped his hands on his tunic, then glanced at the girl. Her back was to him as she cleaned up.

Jacob closed his eyes and quieted his mind, shutting out the sounds around him. He could hear the birds' voices. And then there was another voice — a powerful voice — that drowned out the others.

Jacob felt the shrieking roar in his head, the pain like knives being thrust into his skull. He gritted his teeth and tried to hang on. Pain ripped through him, clouding his vision. All he could see was red and spots of black. He tried to push away the sound, the way he had the birds. Slowly the shriek reduced to a scream that echoed inside his head. Only then did he realize that the scream was actually a word.

Thief!

Jacob sent a thought to the voice. *Please — can you talk more quietly? I haven't stolen anything from you.*

Thief! Murderer! the voice shrieked.

The thoughts echoed through Jacob, so that even his bones seemed to hurt. Somehow, Jacob knew the voice was also in pain. He felt it, like a long deep gash in his side.

Dimly Jacob heard a groaning, and he knew it was his own voice.

If you tell me what was stolen, maybe I can help. The pain was making him feel sick again. He imagined feathers — thousands of feathers — piling onto the voice, making it quieter.

Men, the voice cried. *Always hurting and thieving and tricking.*

Jacob realized the voice was the dragon, the dragon he'd been searching for. Jacob could almost see her in his mind — gleaming silver and blue scales. Wide sturdy wings that held her aloft. Bright, angry eyes. A mouth that breathed flame.

I am not trying to trick you, Jacob sent. *Look into my mind. You'll see I speak the truth.*

Jacob's skin grew warm. He felt as if nails were being driven into his eyes, his skull. An image of a glowing white stone formed in his mind. Jacob knew he'd seen it before. Only where? It was hard to think through the haze of pain.

Then a shriek ripped through Jacob, a cry of pure agony.

You've seen it! the voice cried. *You took it! Lying child of man. Thief!*

No, Jacob sent back, *someone showed it to me.* Jacob remembered now. The dying crow had shown him the image of the stone.

A bird showed you? You talk to birds? The voice lowered, sounding almost curious.

Yes. Or they talk to me. What had the crow said? That Lord Manning's men could control the dragon with the stone. . . .

No one can control me! cried the voice. Her rage was like molten metal eating through Jacob's mind.

Jacob wanted to scream, but couldn't. *Please — your voice is so loud — I'm trying to help.*

Pah. A little thing like you, help me? But the voice got quieter.

I think I know who took your stone, Jacob said. *Or at least, I think I know where it is. I will get it back for you.*

Why would you do that? The voice sounded cold. Distant.

Jacob was not sure what to answer. The dragon wouldn't care about the Dark Times. She wouldn't care that people were suffering. So Jacob sent what he deeply felt. *Because men wronged you. I want to make it right.*

Hmm. The dragon didn't seem to believe him.

I will get back what was stolen from you, Jacob told the dragon. He didn't know how he'd do it, but he knew that he had to try.

You promise? The dragon's voice grew fainter.

I promise.

I will take you up on your promise, child of man. But you mustn't fail. You mustn't fail!

Jacob had done it! He'd actually spoken with a dragon, the last living dragon. Jacob smiled through his haze of pain. He felt almost drunk with joy.

And child of man? Stop calling it a stone, the dragon demanded.

What should I call it, then?

Call it what it is, the dragon snapped. *It's an egg. My egg. Lord Manning stole my egg!*

CHAPTER FIVE | **The Wounded Dragon**

No wonder the dragon was so angry. It was a mother dragon, trying to protect her baby. All mothers were fierce when it came to protecting their own. Now the dragon's rage made sense.

Jacob opened his eyes slowly. The world was blurry at first, and then sharpened. Trees reached up to the sky.

Lia stared down at Jacob, her face pale. Orson hovered behind her, looking grim. Birds flew all around, fluttering near Jacob's face, then darting away again.

I'm all right, Jacob sent to the birds.

A few birds landed on Jacob's head and his shoulders.

45

They were light, like pine cones, and somehow they felt comforting. He laughed.

Orson and Lia grinned back at him. Jacob had survived. Now he was back in the world of the moment.

The moment was full of danger. The three of them had camped in one place too long. If they stayed any longer, Lord Manning's men would surely find them.

But Jacob's arms and legs felt like they were made of lead. Jacob rubbed his face, trying to make himself move. His skin was sticky.

"Wait," Lia said. She pressed a damp rag beneath his nose and wiped down to his chin. The rag came away red. She wiped again.

"You bled. From your nose," Lia said. "How are you feeling now?"

Dizzy, Jacob thought. He had a raging headache, but he felt happy. He'd found the dragon. He'd spoken with her. No one could laugh at him now.

"I'm fine," Jacob lied. "We should get going."

Lia looked at him, concerned. "Are you sure you're okay?"

"I am — but you look pale."

She pressed her lips tightly together. "I grow weak when I use too much power to heal. So, clearly, do you …

when you speak to a dragon. I was worried you might die."

"And that mattered to you?"

"Of course. As the Dragon Speaker, the Chosen One, you can bring the Dark Times to an end. According to the prophecy," Lia said.

The prophecy. How could Jacob have forgotten? Of course Lia didn't care about him. She cared about the prophecy and ending the Dark Times.

In the distance, hoof beats sounded. They were heavy on the damp earth.

Jacob froze, hardly daring to breathe. Beside him, Orson and Lia had grown just as still.

The sounds came closer. Men shouted, their voices growing louder. Armor clanged.

Soldiers! Jacob thought. *Lord Manning's soldiers are searching the area.* Jacob could see glimpses of the men through the trees. And if Jacob could see them. . . . His skin prickled.

The fire crackled and Jacob sucked in his breath. The fire was like a flag waving "Here we are!"

Slowly, trying not to make a sound, Jacob limped to the fire. He threw dirt on it, praying the men wouldn't see any smoke.

Orson gripped his sword so tightly his knuckles were white. His face was tense.

Jacob, Orson and Lia hid together behind some bushes. Waiting.

One of the horses came to a stop only a few trees away. Jacob forgot to breathe.

"You smell smoke?" one man shouted to another.

"It couldn't be them. No one would be stupid enough to light a fire when they're being hunted. Besides, I heard the boy is lame—how could he make it this far?"

Sweat trickled down Jacob's back.

"We could take a rest," the man said.

"Not worth the risk. Lord Manning and Kain would have our necks if they caught us."

"I guess." The first man clucked to his horse, and the two men rode away. Soon the others followed.

Jacob let his breath out. He didn't speak for many minutes. At last, he whispered, "That was close. Thank goodness those knights didn't see us."

Orson spat on the ground. "Those men aren't real knights. They're just hired thugs. Real knights would never hunt innocent people. Or work for someone as cruel as Lord Manning. When I'm a knight, I'll fight for King Harold — or someone as good as him. Someone who cares about people. I'll fight to stop tyrants like Lord Manning."

Lia shivered and rubbed her arms. "The lord before

Manning might have been greedy, but at least he didn't kill people for their magic."

Lia wasn't a spy, Jacob knew that now. She'd been just as afraid of the lord's men as Jacob had been. Perhaps she really was a dragon healer, like she'd said.

Jacob felt a shadow cross his mind, then the roaring voice of the dragon. He looked up through the branches. He couldn't see the dragon yet, but he knew she was very close.

"The dragon's coming," he told the others.

"What?" Orson cried. "How soon? Where is it?" Orson stood up and drew his sword.

Lia jumped up as well. She whirled on Orson. "Put your sword away. A dragon is not a creature to be afraid of. Not for a man of good heart."

"I'll decide that for myself," Orson said stiffly.

"You'll do as I say!" Lia shouted. "Do you have years of dragon training? Do you?" Lia's eyes flashed. She looked like a wild creature ready to attack.

Orson shook his head.

"Then put your sword away," Lia said. "You don't ever want to make a dragon angry."

Jacob laughed. Lia was so right. An angry dragon was too much for any of them — but especially one young man and a sword.

The branches above them began to sway and creak. Birds flew away, screeching. The tree branches moved back to make a wide opening to the cloudy sky. And then the sky was filled with glittering silver and blue. The sound of giant wings filled the air.

I am here, the dragon sent to Jacob, her mind voice loud. The ground shuddered as she landed.

The dragon smelled like fire, stone and iron. And she was big — bigger than any creature Jacob had ever seen. Bigger than ten deer put together. She took up most of the space in the clearing.

Jacob felt his legs shake. The dragon was beautiful and dangerous. But she had been hurt. Her side had been sliced open, pink flesh showing through.

"She's wounded," Lia cried, her voice shaking. She placed her hands on the dragon's side.

Jacob was sure that the dragon could kill them all even if she were injured. Her sharp claws were as big as any man's sword. Orson stood pressed up against a tree, staring with wide eyes.

The dragon turned her head. Her yellow-gold eyes focused on Jacob.

Jacob swallowed hard. He tried to imagine thousands of feathers landing all over the dragon, hoping to soften her voice.

You brought a Dragon Healer? the dragon sent. *Perhaps there is hope for you after all.* The voice rumbled through Jacob's mind, but this time it did not hurt.

Birds fluttered back to the clearing. Some of them carefully approached the dragon.

The dragon brought her large head down to peer at a sparrow that landed near her foot. The dragon made a soft tek-teking sound in Jacob's mind, and Jacob realized she was laughing. *Well, well. A cousin brave enough to visit. How lovely.* Then she turned back to Jacob. *Come. We must stop these murderers.*

Fire shot out of her mouth, burning the leaves and branches it touched.

Lia turned around, hands trembling. Beads of sweat clung to her forehead. "The dragon has lost a lot of blood. I don't know if I can heal her."

The dragon blew smoke from her nose. *Enough talk. We must leave.*

"She says she has to go," Jacob told the others.

"It will kill her," Lia said.

It doesn't matter. I have no choice. The dragon told Jacob. She struggled to rise.

Jacob ached to see such a creature so weak. *I swore that I would find your egg and bring it back to you,* he sent to her. *Trust me.*

The dragon struggled to rise again.

Slowly, Jacob approached the dragon. Up close, her scales looked like shining metal, though thinner than any Orson's pa could make. *Even I can see you're not fit to travel*, he sent to the dragon.

You don't understand. My egg holds the last male dragon. He must live, or our race will die out. Forever. She clawed the ground, raking up a tree.

Jacob could feel her pain as if it were his own. *I swear to you, we won't let that happen.*

The dragon shuddered. *You must not delay. And you must not fail. The wizard is murdering birds to make my egg hatch faster. I know my baby feels the death of his cousins and wants to help.*

I will not fail, Jacob promised.

The dragon rested her head on the ground and closed her eyes. Her mind voice quieted to just a whisper. *I am trusting you, Dragon Speaker. Trusting you. . . .* And then she was asleep.

Jacob turned to the others. "She'll stay, but she wants us to get her egg back. The egg holds the last dragon — a male."

Lia clapped her hand over her mouth. "Oh Jacob, you must get the egg before it hatches. If Kain kills such a young dragon, it will give him more power than anyone can imagine."

Jacob squared his shoulders. "I won't let him do that."

"Yeah. We won't let that happen," Orson said. "No way am I letting Lord Manning get more power. Jacob and I will find that dragon's egg."

Lia nodded. "I'll stay and keep working to heal her."

Jacob rubbed his jaw. Jacob and Orson were leaving them alone — a wounded dragon and a girl who grew weak when she healed too much. And Lord Manning's men were searching the forests. Jacob turned to Orson. "What about them?" he asked, jutting his chin at Lia and the dragon.

Orson pointed over their heads. The tree branches had closed back over them, hiding the sky. "I think she's safe. I think they both are. Who'd look for a dragon here? There aren't even any broken branches." Orson lifted his pack and put his sword in its scabbard.

Lia watched Jacob with her large green eyes. Jacob lifted his own pack to his shoulders and nodded. Lia gave him a nervous smile. "Good luck, Dragon Speaker."

CHAPTER SIX | Inside the Castle

"How many days' walk to the castle?" Jacob asked. He and Orson had been walking through the forest for hours. Now the sun was setting.

"One more day. Maybe a half day if we can push ourselves faster." Orson glanced at Jacob's weak leg.

Jacob clenched his teeth. "I can go faster. We have to." He picked up the pace, ignoring the pain. Jacob felt his blood pumping through him, his heart beating faster. They *had* to get there in time to save the egg!

The two friends walked all day in the shelter of the trees. Jacob chewed on some cold rabbit when he got hungry. He never let up his pace, even when the pain in his leg became so bad he could hardly think.

But by nightfall, he was limping like an old man. His breath came in short gasps.

Orson put his hand on Jacob's shoulder. "I think we should stop for the night."

Jacob shook him off. "No! We have to keep going." They were not going to fail because of his leg. They were not.

"Jacob, your leg looks like it's really hurting," Orson said.

"Well, it's not," Jacob lied.

"Let me see."

Jacob shook his head. "Since when did you become my personal healer?"

Orson's face flushed. He blew out his breath loudly. "Look, if you wreck your leg now you won't be able to save anyone. Remember, you're the Chosen One."

Jacob groaned and tugged off his pack. He eased himself down onto his bag and stretched out his leg. Pain shot through him, and his whole leg throbbed.

Orson crouched down and pulled at Jacob's ripped stocking. Jacob's scars were a bright red instead of their normal pink. They looked like knife slashes against his skin.

Jacob knew his leg was more swollen than normal. He waited for Orson to say something, but his friend didn't speak. Instead, Orson began tearing a strip off the bottom of his tunic.

"What are you doing?"

"I'm no healer," Orson said, "But I can tell your leg isn't right. When my brother twisted his ankle, it got swollen like this. The healer wrapped it up tight. So let's try it." Orson wound the strip of cloth firmly around Jacob's ankle, then tied it.

The pain lessened. Jacob stood to test his leg — and it could bear his weight. He smiled at Orson. "You're better than a healer!"

"I have my moments," Orson said, looking pleased with himself. "But I still think we should call it a night. We've made good time already."

Jacob shook his head. "Every hour we wait gives Kain more time to hatch the egg. I say we keep moving on."

Orson shook his head, but agreed. The moon was still bright and would light their way. And it was always less dangerous to travel at night.

~

Jacob and Orson got to Lord Manning's castle at dawn. The castle was dark gray, almost black in the early morning light. Its pointed towers thrust into the sky like giant teeth. There was a wide moat around the entire castle, filled with stinking, muddy water.

The castle was quiet and still. Even the birds were strangely silent, as if they knew the castle was an evil place.

Jacob shivered. Now that they were here, he didn't know how they were going to get inside the castle. Or how they would find the dragon's egg, once they got inside.

Then Jacob saw movement near the castle's gate. He grabbed Orson's arm and pointed.

Orson nodded. He whispered in Jacob's ear. "Guards. Two of them. How are we going to get past them?"

"I … uh, I don't know."

"You don't have a plan?" Orson whispered.

Jacob gulped. He kept thinking that he'd see a way into the castle. Or that the birds would speak to him. But that hadn't happened.

"Okay, how about this?" Orson said. "I'll tell the two guards that I want to be a soldier for Lord Manning. Once they let me in, I'll find a way to get you in, too."

"You think the guards will believe you?"

Orson grinned. "It's called charm, Jacob. For me, it works every time."

Orson handed his sword to Jacob. Then he walked out of the woods and toward the castle. He held his hands up high to show he did not have a weapon.

This might just work, Jacob said to himself.

Jacob could see Orson talking to the guards. For a few seconds, things seemed to go well. Orson turned toward the forest, and Jacob could see the big smile on his face.

Then something seemed to go wrong. One guard shook his head, then threw Orson against the castle wall. The other guard drew his sword, pointing the tip right against Orson's neck.

Jacob's heart clenched tight as a walnut. With just a quick thrust, his friend could die. The guards might kill him for sport, or because he made them angry, or for no reason at all.

Jacob couldn't let that happen. Carefully, silently, he raised his bow and strung an arrow. He'd never killed a man before, but now so much was at stake.

Jacob drew back the string and aimed at the guard holding the sword. If he aimed this right, Orson would be saved. If he was off, even just a little, his friend would surely die. But what choice did he have?

Jacob released the arrow. It shot through the air,

straight and silent, right at the guard holding his sword at Orson's neck. In seconds, the arrow plunged into the guard's chest. The man fell to the ground, his blood spurting.

The other guard whirled around, drawing his sword. He looked for the archer with such deadly aim. He didn't see Orson bend down and grab the first guard's sword. Nor did he see the thrust that sent him, too, to the bloody ground.

Jacob limped forward and joined Orson, handing him his own sword. Orson dropped the guard's bloody sword.

"I'm glad your aim was good," Orson told him.

"What happened?" Jacob asked. "I thought you were going to talk your way inside."

Orson tried to smile. "I guess I'm not as charming as I thought. Come on. Let's move."

Jacob pulled out another arrow and strung it on the bow, keeping it ready. Orson kept his sword unsheathed. Together, they walked inside the castle gate.

Jacob wished it was still dark enough to hide. But the castle still seemed asleep. There was no one moving, no sounds of morning work.

Then two guards came marching around the corner. "Halt! Stop where you are!" one shouted. Four more guards came running to join them.

Jacob and Orson turned and ran.

"Sound the alarm!"

A shrill bell clanged in the air. More guards streamed out of the upper castle.

Soon there were archers on the roof, aiming for them. An arrow hit a bird. Pain tore through Jacob as it fell to the ground. Jacob shot at the archer and missed. An arrow flew by Jacob's side, ripping through his tunic.

Fly away! Jacob ordered the birds. The birds rose higher, but wouldn't leave.

An arrow hit Jacob in the shoulder, pushing him back with the impact. He screamed.

"Jacob!" Orson cried.

Jacob gritted his teeth and pulled the arrow out. He clenched his teeth so hard pain shot through his jaw. Spots of light danced in front of his eyes. It couldn't end like this! It couldn't end with Jacob and Orson being killed by Lord Manning's men. Not with Jacob failing, again.

"No!" he screamed, his voice ringing out.

As Jacob's scream died away, the sky grew dark with birds. Birds poured from the clouds and treetops like hail. Their sharp cries screeched on and on like an ungodly chorus. The beating of their wings sounded like drums.

In wave after wave, the birds fell upon the guards. The birds pecked at the men's eyes, necks, and hands.

Another arrow struck Jacob's wounded arm, and he dropped his bow. His arm hung uselessly at his side. He tore out the second arrow, hot blood flowing down his arm. There was no way he could shoot an arrow now. So Jacob pulled his dagger from its sheath with his other hand and charged the guards. Birds surrounded him like armor. He fought alongside the birds, grateful for them.

Off to one side, he saw Orson fighting two men at once. *Help him!* Jacob screamed to the birds.

A group of birds tore through the sky, crying harshly. They attacked the men Orson was fighting and drove them back. The remaining guards were starting to look afraid. Some turned and ran. Others lay on the ground, groaning.

"You know," Jacob shouted to Orson, "We might actually win this thing!"

"We *are* winning!" Orson replied.

The remaining guards formed a circle around Orson and Jacob. Jacob could see raw fear in their eyes. They were afraid of the birds and these boys who controlled them.

But then two men began walking from the castle.

"Out of my way!" one of them ordered, and the soldiers gave way.

Lord Manning pushed his way forward. His face was flushed, his blue eyes as cold as the stone of the castle. A silk cloak swirled around him, fastened at his neck by a ruby set in gold. Behind him came a man in a black cloak — the wizard Kain.

Kain locked eyes with Jacob, and the old man smiled thinly. "So we meet again, boy. It looks like I should have killed you the first time." He pointed at Jacob, and started saying words Jacob had heard only once before — when Kain had set fire to his house.

Lord Manning clutched Kain's arm. "Not yet! We need some answers first."

Kain stopped.

Thinking quickly, Jacob flung his dagger at the wizard.

Kain whispered, then closed his hand. The dagger dropped to the grass. "Did you really think that could harm me?"

Jacob felt sick. He and Orson had no weapons left.

"You will stop the birds," Lord Manning said, waving at the attacking birds.

"Or what?" Orson demanded.

Lord Manning smiled grimly. "Or I will have my men

destroy the dragon's egg."

He nodded at the wizard. Kain raised his arms and muttered a spell. The air around Kain began to glow and crackle. An image appeared — two soldiers standing over a large white egg. Their swords were held inches above the egg, ready to plunge into it.

"You know I can do it — the shell is weak," Lord Manning said.

Jacob stared with horror. The thin shell looked almost like parchment. He could see a shadow moving slowly inside the egg. Lord Manning was right.

"I will order it done — unless you do as I say," Lord Manning said, his lips curling into a cruel smile.

CHAPTER SEVEN | "If You're Lucky, You'll Die Quickly."

Lord Manning stepped closer to Jacob. The castle loomed darkly behind him. The birds kept diving and clawing at the guards.

"Call off your demon birds!" Lord Manning shouted.

Stop! Jacob told the birds.

The birds didn't listen.

Jacob looked at Lord Manning and knew he had to do something. He drew into that quiet place inside himself. *STOP!* he sent to the birds.

All around him, the flutter of wings and cries of birds

stopped. Birds settled to the ground, their wings still. Jacob opened his eyes. *No! Fly away. Go!* he sent to them.

As one, the birds rose to the air and flew away. Lord Manning's men watched, open mouthed. Some crossed themselves.

Orson whirled on Jacob. "What are you doing? We were *winning!*" he hissed.

Jacob shook his head.

The soldiers yanked Jacob's arms behind his back. Jacob winced. Another soldier grabbed Orson's arms. "Stop talking!" they demanded.

"Bring them to the Great Hall," Lord Manning ordered. He walked away and the wizard followed him.

The soldiers shoved Jacob and Orson forward, into the dark mouth of the castle. The air inside was chilly. The only light came from flickering torches and narrow slits of windows. Ornate carvings of dragons and knights stood out from the smooth stone. Dark red cloth the color of dried blood hung from the walls.

The soldiers marched Jacob and Orson up a narrow staircase, then down a hallway lined with weapons. They stopped at two heavy black doors. A guard rapped on the door with the grip of his sword.

"Bring them in!"

The soldiers pushed the doors open and dragged Jacob and Orson inside. The room was longer than it was wide, and paintings hung along the walls. A gold throne stood at the far end.

A *throne*, Jacob thought. *Only the King should sit on such a throne.*

Lord Manning stood in front of the throne, looking down at them. His narrow face was handsome if you didn't look at his cold eyes or his hard mouth. The wizard Kain stood beside him, the teeth of his victims shining in his dark hair.

"You may go," Lord Manning told the soldiers.

As the men left, bolting the door behind them, Lord Manning seated himself on the throne. He turned his gaze on Jacob. "Why are you here, boy?"

"We've come to … to ask you to show mercy on our village," Jacob said.

"Nonsense," Lord Manning replied. He pushed his fingers together. "Kain tells me you're after my dragon egg."

How does the wizard know that? Jacob wondered. Sweat pricked Jacob's back. What else might Lord Manning know?

"How did you find out about my egg?" Lord Manning demanded. "Who told you?"

"No one," Jacob said.

Lord Manning snorted. "Come, come. You can do better than that."

"We're not after your egg," Jacob said. And that was the truth. He was after the *dragon's* egg; it wasn't Lord Manning's.

"Besides, what would we do with it?" Orson threw in.

"What indeed," Lord Manning said, arching his eyebrows. He turned a jeweled ring on his finger. "I see you boys have spirit. That's so rare these days — given how easily I can have you both killed."

The wizard Kain stepped forward. "Tell us how you controlled those birds. If you answer honestly, we will let you live." His eyes bore into Jacob's.

"It's not magic."

"Another lie!" Lord Manning said.

The wizard muttered a few words and snapped his fingers. Sparks danced, and then a red flame appeared. It flickered and turned white.

The wizard spoke again, and the flame disappeared. "He's telling the truth," Kain said.

"A pity." Lord Manning stroked his lips. "I don't suppose you can get me the boy's power, anyway?"

"I'd love to try," the wizard said, and grinned. His sharp white teeth gleamed like splinters of bone. "Most people will give up anything after a bit of pain."

"You can have your way with him later — when I'm through," Lord Manning said.

Jacob felt sick. Take his powers? Could they? He glanced at Orson. Orson's huge shoulders were hunched, and his face was tight. He was scared, Jacob realized.

Lord Manning brought his steepled fingers to his mouth. "I'll ask you one more time. How did you know about my dragon's egg? And you'd better answer honestly, boy — or your friend will discover what pain means."

"I dreamt it," Jacob answered quickly.

"You dreamt it?" Lord Manning's eyelids flickered. "What else did you dream, boy?"

"I dreamt that you died on your knees, begging for mercy," Jacob replied.

Lord Manning roared. He leapt out of his chair, fingers curling into a fist.

The wizard caught his arm. "My Lord! The boy is toying with you. If that were in your future, I would have seen it."

Lord Manning growled and sank back onto his throne. "I'll give you the boy, the one who controls birds. Do what you want with him." He paused, then eyed Orson up and down. "You, young man — you look like a strong, sensible lad. How would you like a place in my castle, as one of my soldiers? Who knows; if you're good enough, you might train as a knight."

Orson spat. "I'd rather die."

"Then you'll get your wish," Lord Manning barked. "Kain. . . ."

Before he could finish, the hall doors burst open.

"What is the meaning of all this?" Lord Manning shouted.

A man in riding clothes bowed deeply. He was out of breath. "Sorry, my Lord, but you wanted to know as soon as the dragon was sighted. . . ."

Jacob's chest tightened.

Lord Manning's eyes brightened. *Oh no!* The wizard licked his lips.

"At last!" Lord Manning said. "Guards!" he bellowed. "Take these two to the dungeon." He gave them a dark look. "We'll deal with you later."

Two guards came in and yanked Jacob and Orson out of the room. They pushed the boys roughly down the hall, then down a winding set of stairs. The stairs seemed to go on forever, plunging deeper into the damp darkness.

Jacob heard a faint humming in his head as he walked. The humming felt like an echo of the dragon. It must be the egg! They were getting closer, even if they had no choice.

"This is good!" Orson said. "At least we postponed our deaths. It gives us a chance to escape. A true knight never gives up, you know."

"Yeah, but I think they found … the one we were hiding," Jacob said softly. "And that means they must have Lia, too. There's nothing good about that."

"Quiet, you!" the guard said and hit Jacob on the side of his head.

Jacob stumbled, losing his balance. Orson shot out his hand and caught Jacob to steady him.

"Keep moving!" the guard ordered.

They went down more stairs in silence. Jacob heard a steady drip. The air grew colder the deeper they got.

"We have to go rescue them!" Jacob whispered.

"We need rescuing ourselves," Orson replied. He got a smack on his head as well.

At last they reached the bottom of the stairs. The dim hall stretched out in a straight line on both sides. The guards shoved Jacob and Orson to the right.

The halls here weren't carved of smooth stone, like those in the palace. The stone here was roughly cut, like a tunnel that had been hacked right out of the rock. Torches flickered on the walls, casting shadows. Jacob felt as if the stone were pressing all around him, making it hard to breathe.

They reached the end of the hall. Jacob saw the cell, now. It was dark, but he could see that three walls were made of thick stone, and one wall was an iron grate. Dirty straw littered the floor. Rats squealed, scurrying around. There was the stench of unwashed bodies and fear.

One guard took a ring of keys off a peg on the wall. He unlocked the door and yanked it open. Then he shoved the two boys in, clanging the door shut behind them.

"The wizard likes to take his time with people who anger him," the guard said. "If you're lucky, you'll die quickly."

The key turned in the lock with a final clink. The two guards walked away, talking to each other. Their footsteps and laughter echoed down the hall, then faded into silence.

Jacob sank down onto the straw to give his weak leg a rest, and he flexed his injured arm. It was getting better.

"So I have some company at last," a creaky voice said from the darkness. "To what do I owe this pleasure?"

CHAPTER EIGHT | A Stranger in the Dungeon

Jacob jumped at the stranger's voice. He hadn't known anyone else was in the cell. "I don't think it takes much to get locked in this dungeon," Jacob said.

"Mmm," the voice replied. "Lord Manning usually kills people right away, or makes them slaves. You must be of special interest to him."

"Not really. Something more important came up," Jacob said. "He'll probably kill us later."

"*I'm* not getting killed." Orson kicked the straw. "But

I don't like this — talking to someone in the dark. Come out where we can see you."

There was a shuffling sound, and then an old man appeared. His white hair stood up all over his head, and his long nose looked like a beak.

The man looked at them from under bushy white eyebrows. "It's always good to be aware of who and what is around you," he said, nodding at Orson. "But you should learn to trust more than just your sense of sight."

The old man turned his gaze to Jacob. His eyes were steady and bright, not like an old man's eyes at all. "And you, young man, should learn how to tell lies better."

Learn to lie better? That's the advice the old man had for him? "Uh … thanks," Jacob replied.

The old man chuckled and reached his hand into his tattered blue robe. He pulled out a flask. "Drink?" he asked, offering it to Jacob, then Orson. "It might lift your spirits."

"No thanks," Jacob said. Jacob noticed the mark of a healer on the man's wrinkled hand.

The old man caught him staring and shook his head. "I am a healer no more," the old man said. "Gave it up. Gave up all of that." He shuffled off back into the darkness.

Jacob stared after him. He felt certain the old man

had a lot of secrets. And he wondered if he was telling the truth.

Orson paced up and down the length of the cell.

Jacob turned away, clutched the bars and stared gloomily out. The humming in his mind grew louder. He was sure it was the egg, calling to him. Yet now he was stuck in a cell, unable to help. Were Lia and the dragon okay? Or had Lord Manning's men found them?

Orson brushed by Jacob.

"Pacing isn't going to get us out of here!" Jacob snapped.

"Neither is staring at the wall," Orson answered back and kept pacing.

Jacob turned back to the bars. Orson was right. If only he had some useful magic. But no, all he could do was talk to birds. And dragons.

Hours passed. Jacob's stomach rumbled, but neither he nor Orson wanted to eat the little rabbit meat they had left. The torches flickered. One or two went out. Some new guards came, bringing new torches. The old man snored loudly in the darkness. Then Orson was asleep, too. Finally Jacob lowered himself onto the dirty straw that barely covered the cold floor. Maybe he'd been wrong, telling the birds to stop. Maybe he should have kept on fighting. Jacob shifted to one side and tried to sleep.

~

Jacob woke to the squeal of hinges and the clang of metal against stone. The humming in his head started up again, even louder than the night before. He jerked upright, his body cold and aching.

A guard leered in at him. "Eat well — it could be your last meal."

Jacob looked down. Three metal bowls held gray, lumpy cereal with spoons sticking upright. Though his stomach ached with hunger, Jacob wasn't sure he would be able to keep it down.

Orson sat up groaning. "That floor is worse than the ground on a cold night," he said.

"Breakfast already?" the old man said, tottering into the light.

Jacob nodded at the dishes. The old man picked up a bowl with his gnarled hands and started gulping down the cereal.

Orson picked up a bowl and brought a spoonful to his lips. "Not too bad," he said thoughtfully. "Better than my pa makes."

Jacob shook his head. He still didn't want to eat the mess. All he wanted was to get out of here.

Orson scraped his bowl clean and burped. "You going to eat yours?"

"No," Jacob said. "Help yourself."

Orson looked at him. "You got a plan?"

"No," Jacob said. He rubbed his forehead.

"What's wrong? You hear something?" Orson asked.

"It's like the egg is talking to me," Jacob said. "Like it wants me to find it." Jacob stared out through the bars. The key to the cell hung on the wall, so close he could almost reach it. It taunted him. If only Jacob had magic. Or something to make the key fly into his hands.

Wait — could he get a bird to fly the key to him? Could it be as simple as that?

Jacob reached inside himself. *Birds — come! I need you.*

He looked through the bars down the hall, toward the stairs. No bird appeared.

Jacob closed his eyes and concentrated. *Birds — I need you! Come!* He sent his thought as hard as he could.

Still nothing.

"Filth and maggots!" Jacob shouted, shaking the bars.

"You were talking to the birds, weren't you?" Orson said.

"Yeah, but they didn't listen," Jacob said bitterly.

The old man spoke up from the shadows. "That was you causing the uproar the other day, was it?"

"Uh, yeah."

The old man shuffled into the faint light to peer at Jacob. His eyes were wide. "Can you really talk to birds, boy?"

Should he tell the truth? Jacob glanced over at Orson. Orson shrugged.

"Yes," Jacob said.

"I'd like to see that, I would."

"I'm trying, but they don't seem to listen. It's still pretty new to me — asking them to do something."

"Hmm." The old man sounded curious. "What are you asking them to do?"

"To fly in here, take the key off the wall, and hand it to me."

"Isn't all that a bit much — for a bird?" Orson asked.

"Birds are smart!" Jacob said, whirling on him. "Crows pick up shiny objects all the time and carry them to their nests."

The old man cleared his throat. "How are you talking to them?"

"How?" Jacob's forehead wrinkled.

"Are you asking them in words? Pictures?"

"Oh, I see. Words."

"And when they came to your aid yesterday, how did they know you needed them?"

"I don't know. I was angry, and then they just came."

"Hmm." The old man scratched his tunic. His nails sounded loud on the rough fabric. "Why don't you use your emotion, your need, when you call them. And use mind pictures. Before a child learns to talk, he knows the meaning of images. I suspect birds are like that."

Jacob was surprised at the thought, but it felt right. He closed his eyes and focused on how much he needed to get out of the dungeon. How afraid he was for Lia. How much he needed to save the egg.

Fear pumped through Jacob. Slowly, he built up an image in his mind of a crow flying through the doors and down the winding stairs. He held those images in his mind as if time slowed down, and then sent them with his fear.

A moment later, he heard the beating of wings.

"Jacob!" Orson whispered. "Look."

Jacob opened his eyes to see a crow flying down the hall. *Dragon Speaker, you called me?*

Yes. Please — bring me the key. Jacob pictured the crow unhooking the key from the wall and clasping it in its beak. Then he pictured the bird placing the key in his hand.

Almost as soon as he sent the images, the crow was doing exactly as he'd imagined. Jacob held the cold iron key in his hand and looked at it with wonder. *Thank you,* he sent.

The crow nodded and flew away. Jacob fit the key in the lock and turned it.

"That was amazing!" the old man said.

"Even better will be getting out of here ... without getting caught," Jacob replied.

"Oh, you will." The old man looked at Jacob. "I have no doubt about it."

Well, I have my doubts, Jacob thought. He pushed the cell door. The metal hinges squealed as they opened.

"You're free now, too," Jacob said to the old man.

The old man put his hand on Jacob's shoulder. "Thank you, son. What is your name?"

"Jacob."

"Jacob. From which village?"

"Maldon." He didn't know why the old man was asking him so many questions, but he didn't have time to think about them. "Come on, Orson! We have to get the egg!"

Orson slipped past the old man. "Nice meeting you, sir. You might want to get out of here before the guards get back."

"Oh, I will," the old man said, but he didn't step out of the prison cell. "My name is Aldous, and I am in your debt. I won't forget it. Ever."

Jacob waved to the old man, then hurried down the hall. He followed the humming noise in his mind, hoping it would lead to the egg. He and Orson walked down the hall the way they'd come.

They passed a room full of weapons with no one guarding them. Jacob stopped. "We'd better grab a few of these. I think we'll need them."

Orson took down a sword, testing its weight.

Jacob reached for one as well. It was so heavy it threw him off balance. His face hot, he glanced at Orson. Orson was busy with his own sword and didn't seem to have noticed.

Sighing, Jacob walked over to the daggers. He put one in his belt and one beneath his leg strap. Then he took down a quiver of arrows and the smallest bow he could find. The bow was much thicker and heavier than the one he was used to, but he thought he'd be able to use it.

The humming in his head was getting louder, more intense. He felt some birds, too — trapped, scared birds. They made his head ache.

"Come on," Jacob said and started down the hall as fast as he could.

The hall curved at the end, and there was more light

the further they went. They passed several empty rooms. Now the humming was so loud Jacob almost felt as if the egg was right in front of him. Jacob slid to a halt before an open doorway. Orson stopped beside him, waiting.

Jacob cautiously stuck his head around the doorway and peered in. This room was big — large enough to be a banquet room. Lit torches lined the walls, brightening the room, but shadows still crept into the corners. A scarred wooden table and chairs stood to one side, with a half-eaten meal laid out. There were thick slices of meat, piles of grapes, hunks of crusty bread and golden cheese. Jacob swallowed, trying to ignore his hunger. Along one wall were cages of birds — more kinds of birds than Jacob had ever seen. Jacob could feel their fear, but their thoughts were too frantic to make out.

Something wasn't right. Something in the room wasn't right.

Jacob looked past the table. And there it was: the egg, the dragon's egg, up on a raised platform. The egg was large, as big as two men's heads, and its shell was thin. Inside was a moving shadow — the last of the male dragons.

The room looked empty, but the egg was there. Where were the guards?

Jacob crept into the room, Orson behind him. Jacob had just reached out his hand toward the egg when he heard the voice.

"Ha! I knew if I took the guards away, you'd try to steal my egg!"

CHAPTER NINE | So Much Blood

Jacob spun around to see Lord Manning jump from behind the cages of birds. His wizard was behind him.

"Kain — stop them," Lord Manning ordered.

"Gladly." Kain laughed — a cackling, unpleasant laugh — and stepped out of the shadows. His black robe fluttered.

"You can't stop us!" Orson shouted.

The wizard muttered a few words. He raised his hand, pointing at Jacob.

Jacob flew back through the air and hit the wall,

hard. Jacob groaned and struggled to stand, but he felt stunned.

Orson lifted his sword and yelled. The wizard pointed at Orson and whispered some strange words. The sword flew out of Orson's hand, as if an invisible giant had torn it away. Orson's arms hung empty at his side.

Jacob staggered up, his muscles aching. He picked up his bow and arrow, trying to fit the arrow on its string. But the wizard muttered more words, flicked his fingers, and the arrow fell to the ground. Kain flicked his fingers again, and the bow and arrows tore out of Jacob's hands. They smashed into the wall and splintered.

The wizard smiled, his sharp teeth grinning. "What now, boy?"

Lord Manning looked gleeful. "Make them hurt!"

Jacob looked around wildly. The birds clamored in their cages, wanting to help, but there were too many cages to open. And he'd never reach the birds before Kain stopped him. He had to find another way.

Jacob watched the wizard in case he uttered any more spells. That gave Jacob an idea. "Get ready to tackle Kain," he whispered to Orson.

Jacob started for the table at an uneven run. "Food! I need food!" Jacob yelled, diving for the bread.

Lord Manning just laughed. "This is the boy who's supposed to defeat me?"

"He's up to something!" Kain said. "Stop! "

But Jacob was too fast for him. He rammed the piece of bread into the wizard's open mouth. The wizard's voice was cut off.

"Orson, a little help here!" Jacob yelled.

Orson tackled the wizard to the ground, and Jacob tied Kain's wrists together with his leg strap.

Lord Manning just stood there, amazed. How could two boys – two peasants – overpower his wizard?

"No!" Lord Manning yelled. "You can't do this!"

"We can and we did," Jacob said, taking down the ring of keys for the bird cages. He unlocked a cage and opened it. "You're not so high and mighty without your wizard, are you?"

Lord Manning roared. He pulled a sword off the wall and glared at the two young men.

Jacob turned to see Lord Manning charge at Orson with the gleaming sword. The lord brought his sword down before Orson could even lift his. The blade bit deep into Orson's arm. Blood spurted everywhere.

"Orson!" Jacob cried. He threw himself at the lord, knocking the man over. Birds flew at Lord Manning with a fury, attacking his eyes and face. Lord Manning screamed, trying to fight them off, but the birds trapped him in one corner of the room.

Orson staggered to the wall, then slid to the floor. He clutched his arm. Blood seeped out between his fingers.

"No!" Jacob cried. He ran to Orson and knelt before him. Jacob ripped off a strip of his tunic and held it tightly against Orson's arm. The fabric quickly grew dark red. The smell of blood filled Jacob's nose.

"Don't die on me," Jacob whispered.

Orson stared at him with wide, pleading eyes. Jacob felt useless. Was he going to sit there and watch his friend die? He pressed the cloth harder against Orson's arm.

Orson's eyes started to close. Blood kept seeping through the rough cloth.

Tears burned Jacob's eyes. There had to be something he could do.

Jacob staggered to his feet and limped out to the doorway. With uneven steps he went down the hall, then around the corner.

Aldous was still standing in the cell as if lost in thought.

"I need you now!" Jacob yelled. "If you want to repay your debt, come save my friend."

The old man looked up, then slowly shuffled forward.

Jacob bit his own hand. "Hurry!"

The old man sped up, his gait almost like a young man's. He pushed past Jacob into the room. First he saw Lord Manning struggling against the birds. Then he saw Orson in a pool of blood. Quickly Aldous reached into his robe. The old man pulled out some foul smelling herbs, then ripped the cloth off Orson's arm. He pressed the herbs into Orson's gaping wound and waited.

"Herbs?" Jacob clenched and unclenched his hands, breathing hard. "What good will herbs do?"

"A great deal — along with some magic by a powerful healer," Aldous said, and winked.

Jacob stared at him. Suddenly he knew what the old man meant. Aldous was talking about himself. *He* was the healer.

Orson's eyelids fluttered. There was so much blood — in the cloth, on Orson's clothes, on the floor.

"Orson. . . ."

Orson opened his eyes and sat up, grinning crookedly. "I'm okay."

Jacob looked closer and saw that the wound on Orson's arm had closed. He almost didn't believe it.

Jacob sat back on his heels and stared at Aldous. "Thank you. I don't know what I would have done if—"

The old man stood heavily. "My debt to you is repaid, Jacob of Maldon. Until we three meet again." Then he shuffled out of the room.

Orson staggered to his feet.

Lord Manning was still struggling on the floor. "Have mercy! Call these birds off!" he cried. His face was torn and covered with blood.

Leave him! Jacob sent to the birds and showed them the way in his mind.

The birds stopped pecking and clawing. They flew out the door and down the hall like a stream of ribbons.

Lord Manning sobbed. He did not fight when Jacob took off a belt and tied his wrists with it.

Jacob looked at him with disgust. Then he went and freed the rest of the birds. The birds flew away, all but one. A crow. It remained perched on top of a cage. Jacob wondered if it was the same crow that had helped him earlier.

Over on its stand, the dragon's egg hummed at Jacob.

Jacob walked over and stood looking at the shadow inside the shell. He'd paid such a price to rescue this egg. His best friend, almost killed. New enemies made. And bloodshed, everywhere.

Jacob glanced at Orson. "If you want to leave now, I understand."

"Are you kidding?" Orson said. "A knight never gives up his quest. And we've got the dragon's egg. We're almost done."

Jacob took off his tunic and gently laid the egg inside. The egg was warm — almost hot to the touch.

"You're too late, you know," Lord Manning said. He was spitting out blood.

"What do you mean?" Jacob asked.

"We sent the dragon to destroy your village. She's burning it down right now. I doubt any of your people will survive."

Jacob staggered back. "No!"

Lord Manning laughed, blood dripping from his face. "Yes. All those people dead — all because of you. Your dragon gave in, boy. She didn't want us crushing her egg. So now you have no home. And all those deaths are on your hands."

"Don't listen to him," Orson said. "He's just trying to trick you."

"There's no trick. You'll see soon enough," said Lord Manning.

Jacob reached out with his mind to the dragon. *Don't hurt the village! Please!*

The dragon didn't respond.

The crow still sat on top of the cage. Jacob bit his lip and had an idea.

Warn them! Jacob sent to the birds. *Warn the villagers. Please!*

The crow cocked its head. It preened a feather, then flew out the door without answering. Jacob didn't know if the bird had understood him or not.

Jacob felt numb. He hefted the egg in its tunic sling over his shoulder. Then he and Orson made their way up from the cellar, keeping an eye out to avoid the guards. As they neared the stables, Orson stopped. "A horse would be faster."

Jacob nodded.

Orson saddled a horse and Jacob scrambled up on the saddle, feeling clumsy. He placed the egg on his lap. Orson climbed in front of him and took the reins.

All Jacob could think about was his home. His father, who was always angry with him but was still his father. Orson's pa, who always had a kind word for Jacob. And all the villagers who had died … because of him.

If Lord Manning was telling the truth. But why wouldn't he be?

Jacob had been trying to protect all of them. He'd been trying to stop what Lord Manning would do if he gained more power. Instead, he'd caused something just as evil to happen.

Jacob clenched his teeth. Had he really been trying to protect people? Or had he just been trying to prove himself? He'd wanted the men of Maldon to see that he wasn't useless. He'd wanted his father to see that he didn't need two good legs to be a man. And what had that gotten him and the village? Death and destruction.

"I never should have started this," Jacob sighed.

"We don't know anything yet," Orson said. But his face was tight and strained.

Jacob wondered if anyone would be alive when they reached the village.

CHAPTER TEN | The Dragon's Egg

Jacob and Orson galloped toward the village. Their horse kicked up dust around them. It had taken them over a day to get home, a day of hard riding and close calls on the road.

Let them be alive, Jacob thought, clutching the egg. *Let Lord Manning be a liar.*

As they drew closer, Jacob saw smoke rising above the trees. They came over a hill, and then the village was in front of them — or what was left of it. Burned, smoking rubble lay on the ground. Only a few blackened huts still stood. The village of Maldon — or what was left of it — smelled strongly of charred wood. The place was strangely quiet. Nothing rustled in the leaves. Not even one bird sang.

Orson leapt off the horse and ran to where his pa's blacksmith shop used to be. He knelt in the ashes. All that remained were hunks of twisted iron poking up from the ash.

"Pa!" he cried.

Jacob's eyes burned. He scrambled off the horse. He slung the egg over his back. Blindly he stumbled over to where his father's hut should be. But he already knew that it was gone. Burned to ashes.

Jacob felt like his chest was ripping open. He'd been waiting for years for his father to love him. Now he'd never have that chance.

Birds? Where are you? Jacob could feel their fear, now, but they didn't respond.

Slowly Jacob stood and limped over to Orson. Tears were streaming down Orson's face. He wiped them away with his hands when Jacob came to stand with him.

Anger and pain slashed through Jacob. Gold-tinted images flashed through his mind — villagers surrounded by birds, screaming, running away. And beyond that

image was the dragon. Jacob sent one thought to her. *Dragon? We have your egg.*

A deep groan was the reply. The earth trembled.

"Jacob? Is it . . . ?"

"Yes." Jacob limped toward the forest, the egg slung on his back. Orson followed.

Jacob stepped over the blackened, smoldering trees — and saw the dragon. She wasn't shining any more; she was a deep, dull gray, the color of stone.

"Dragon!" Jacob limped faster. This was the dragon that had killed his father, the dragon that had destroyed his village. He should be angry. He should want revenge. But the dragon had been given no choice. She'd had to give in, to save her baby. The dragon was a victim, too.

Where was Lia? She should be here.

"Lia?" Jacob yelled. "Lia, where are you? We're back!"

The dragon lifted her head weakly, opening her crusted eyelids. Her eyes were a dull yellow. *She fainted, trying to heal me,* the dragon sent to Jacob.

Jacob saw Lia now, lying on the ground near the dragon's foot. Her eyes were closed, her skin pale, but she was breathing. Jacob knelt and touched her cheek. Lia didn't stir.

You have my egg? the dragon asked.

I do. Jacob gently lowered the egg and set it in front of her.

The dragon smiled. *You must look after him for me. Our fate is in your hands.*

This is your baby, Jacob replied. *You can raise him. You're free now.*

No, the dragon sent. *Look at me. The wizard's magic was strong and tainted with blood. I'm dying for what I did. I won't be here to see the birth of my own baby.*

Isn't there anything we can do? Jacob said.

You can promise that you will keep my baby safe.

Jacob hesitated. So much evil had come from this. But it wasn't the dragon's fault. It was Kain's and Lord Manning's. They were greedy, cruel men. Jacob had to show the dragon that humans weren't all like that.

I promise, Jacob answered.

Orson looked back and forth between the dragon and his friend. Of course, he could hear none of their thoughts. "... Jacob?"

Jacob shook his head. He couldn't speak. He'd saved the dragon's egg but failed to save its mother, the villagers, or even his own father. Tears leaked from his eyes. The giant dragon was such a noble creature. A magical one, in a time when people desperately needed magic. And now they were losing even that.

Lord Manning and the wizard had done so much damage. All to keep their power. The dragon didn't deserve to die. Nor did any of the villagers.

The dragon groaned again, her head hitting the ground. The earth shuddered. The dragon's eyes closed. Her color faded to a pale gray. Her sides stopped moving as she took a last breath.

"She's gone," Jacob whispered. "And Lia has almost killed herself trying to heal her."

"Lia will be okay," Orson said.

Jacob nodded. She had to be. He knelt over Lia again and Lia stirred, as if she felt him there. She opened her eyes, pushed herself up on her elbow. "You're here."

"Lia. . . ."

Jacob didn't know how to begin, how to tell her what had happened. In the end, he didn't have to. Lia looked over at the slumped body of the dragon ... and knew.

Jacob looked, too. One of the last great magical creatures was gone from the earth. Forever. And the dragon's poor baby had lost his mother before he was even born.

Jacob put his hand on the egg. It was burning hot. He jumped back.

"What's wrong?" Orson asked.

A loud crack rang through the air. Orson looked around nervously. "What was that?"

The crack sounded again. A dark line appeared on the surface of the egg.

"The egg is hatching," Lia said.

More lines appeared, and then the top of the shell burst off. Fragments of shell flew everywhere.

A little head, the size of a cat's, poked up out of the shell. Its eyes were bright yellow-gold, like its mother's, and its hide was a gleaming silver. It gave a little sneeze. Puffs of smoke escaped from its nostrils.

Lia clapped her hands together, grinning.

The dragon gazed at Jacob with huge eyes. Jacob felt like a hook had been plunged into him, tugging him toward the baby dragon. He couldn't look away.

Momma! Hungry! the baby dragon sent to Jacob.

"Oh, wait, I'm not your. . . ."

"Squawk!" the baby dragon cried. It sounded like an angry bird, flapping its wide wings. His little teeth looked as sharp as those of a wolf.

Jacob felt the dragon's hunger as if it were his own. But Jacob didn't have any food. What did dragons eat, anyway?

Jacob looked around wildly. Orson was staring open

mouthed at the baby dragon. "Orson, do you have any of that rabbit meat left?"

"What?" Orson blinked.

"Rabbit! Do you have any left?"

"Oh, yeah. I think so." Orson fumbled in his pouch and pulled out a piece of meat.

Jacob grabbed it and walked up to the egg.

The baby dragon stretched out his neck and snatched the food out of Jacob's hand. He swallowed the meat in one gulp, then burped.

"Got any more?" Jacob asked.

"Here." Orson shoved another piece at Jacob.

The baby dragon snuffled it, then ate it. The dragon licked his lips, then leaped out of his shell and half flapped, half fell into Jacob's arms. The dragon's skin was warm and leathery. He was light, too, much lighter than he looked. He smelled like smoke, metal and stone.

"Oh, he's such a cutie," Lia crooned. She scratched the dragon's chin.

The baby dragon half-closed his eyes. His mouth curved in what Jacob was sure was a smile.

Birds in the forest began to sing and chirp. They flew to Jacob in waves, some of them landing on his head and arms, others circling around the baby dragon.

Jacob laughed. *Hey, where were you?* he asked the birds. *Why didn't you come when I called?*

The Dragon was angry with pain, a bird sent. *But she is gone now. She has left us.*

The baby dragon squeaked and pushed his face into Jacob's neck. He seemed afraid of the birds.

"Hey, they're your cousins," Jacob said. "They won't hurt you. And you're a lot bigger than they are."

Orson laughed.

The baby dragon snorted a puff of smoke. He sat up, though he still trembled.

Jacob stroked the baby dragon's back. "That's right." He took a deep breath. "Lia, could you look after this little one? I must go . . . bury the dead," he said heavily.

But Jacob never made it down the hill.

CHAPTER ELEVEN | Heroes

Before Jacob could start down the hill, he saw a sight he couldn't believe. The villagers of Maldon were gathered just below, watching him. They were silent and wide eyed, with many blackened faces.

Jacob wondered if they were ghosts. How could they have lived through the fire? How could anyone have survived?

"Orson, do you see what I see?" Jacob whispered, his voice rough.

Orson turned to look. His mouth fell open.

A little girl came up to Jacob and broke the quiet. "You missed it all, Jacob. The birds saved us! They flew and clawed and tugged at us. They made us go with them into the woods."

"Oh. They did, did they?" Jacob smiled. He looked up at the birds who were sitting on the trees. *Thank you, my friends. I owe you.*

The birds sent a reply. *No. You freed us. You stopped the murders. We are even, at least for now.*

"You — you talked to the dragon!" a plump woman said. She looked at Jacob with wide eyes.

"Yes. I did."

"You've saved the baby dragon?" a man said, stepping forward. "Why would you do a fool thing like that? The big one tried to kill us."

"The big dragon," Jacob said, "attacked only when Lord Manning threatened her baby. She could have killed you all, but she didn't. No dragon is your enemy. Your enemy is still in his castle."

"He's right," Orson said. "Listen to my friend."

The villagers shuffled their feet. They looked down at the ground. To speak against Lord Manning was to risk their lives.

Jacob reached up to touch the baby dragon on his shoulder. "This little dragon will not hurt you. Lord

Manning and Kain wanted to kill him, like they did so many of your sons. That should tell you something."

The villagers muttered. Jacob's words were sinking in.

The little girl tugged at Jacob's tunic. "Can I pet him?" she asked.

"Get away from that thing!" a woman shrieked.

Jacob just ignored the woman. "Sure, you can," Jacob told the girl. "Just be gentle, okay? He's only a baby." Jacob knelt down, holding the dragon firmly.

The dragon shivered.

Don't be afraid, Jacob told the dragon. *The girl just wants to see you. She's a young one, like you.*

The baby dragon poked his nose out and nudged the girl's hand. The girl laughed. Lia stepped into the shadow of the trees.

"Orson!" a man shouted. And then Orson's father pushed his way out of the crowd.

Orson ran to him. The two of them hugged, slapping each other's backs.

Orson's pa turned to Jacob. "Jacob," he said gently. "I'm afraid. . . ."

"Is it my father?" But Jacob knew the answer before he asked.

Orson's pa just shook his head. "I'm sorry, Jacob. He wouldn't follow the birds. He. . . ."

Jacob looked away. His father was really dead. Like his mother and brother before him.

Jacob was alone — one young man against a very dark world.

Orson's father turned to his son. "Did you two really fight Lord Manning and the wizard? And save this little dragon?"

"Yes, Pa," Orson said. "Jacob and I did. Jacob can talk to them, you see."

The old man raised his eyebrows as he looked at Jacob. "You're the Dragon Speaker? The one in the prophecy?"

Jacob ducked his head. "Well. . . ."

"People!" Orson's pa shouted to the crowd. "Jacob here is the Dragon Speaker! He and my son fought Lord Manning and the wizard. They saved the dragon's baby."

The villagers listened in silence.

"This is the beginning of the prophecy," Orson's father declared. "It's the beginning of the end of the Dark Times!"

Some villagers nodded. Others' faces lightened.

Then one little boy clapped. Another child joined in. Soon many of the villagers were clapping and shouting. "Jacob!" "Our hero!"

"And Orson and Lia! They're heroes, too!" Jacob told them.

Orson walked up beside Jacob. "Don't worry about glory for us. We know the real story. That's what counts."

"Yeah. . . ."

"I'm going to help you protect the dragon, you know," Orson told him. "After we rebuild the village."

Jacob smiled. "I know. I wouldn't have it any other way."

Lia joined them, and they stood together — the three of them and the little dragon. Jacob felt their strength, solid as stone. All his family was gone, but that didn't mean he had to face the world alone.

Lia smiled at him. There was a sweetness in her smile that he'd never seen before. Suddenly everything felt right. Jacob breathed in deeply and lifted his head to the sun.

But then the air in front of Jacob began to shimmer. There was a burst of color and then a fuzzy image. The wizard Kain's face appeared, growing sharper. Lord Manning hovered behind him.

Jacob looked around. No one else seemed to see the image. It was a message for him and him alone.

Kain bared his teeth. *Boy — you may think you've won, but this is only the beginning. You have no idea what I can do. I will take that dragon from you, whether you're alive or dead. You have already lost.*

The image flickered, then faded.

"I'll be ready, Kain," Jacob muttered. "Whenever I see you next."

"Who're you talking to?" Orson asked.

Jacob looked at all the happy faces around him, then at the blackened village. They had a lot of work ahead of them. They had to keep the baby dragon safe from Lord Manning. They had to fight the spells of the wizard Kain. And they had to rebuild their village. But that was later. For now, he just let Orson enjoy the sweetness of their success.

"Oh, no one," Jacob answered. "No one at all."

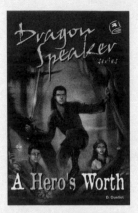

A HERO'S WORTH
by D.M. Ouellet

Book Two of the
Dragon Speaker Series

Jacob and Orson must prove their worth in the battle against Lord Manning. Just as the baby dragon begins to grow, Lia is taken prisoner by her own father and will soon be forced to marry Lord Manning.

Jacob and Orson vow to rescue her. Orson manages to enter the castle to compete at the Samain Festival. He lets Jacob inside and the two combine to take on Lord Manning and his wizard, Kain. The battle is violent, with terrible injuries to both sides. Near the end, Kain is reaching into Jacob's mouth to extract a tooth — to add to his trophies — when there is a noisy surprise.

ISBN 978-1-897039-47-2
www.hip-books.com/fantasy
A teacher's guide is available to cover all three novels.

DRACO'S FIRE
by E.L. Thomas

Book Three of the
Dragon Speaker Series

To fulfill the prophecy, Jacob must bring together the two parts of the comet stone. Jacob expects his friend Orson to help, but Orson betrays him. Soon Lord Manning has both Orson and Lia under his control. He's ready to force Lia into marriage.

Jacob has only his own courage, and Draco the fully grown dragon, on his side. But the comet returns, and magic can sometimes work miracles. Draco's fire is only one part of a spectacular finish to the Dragon Speaker trilogy.

ISBN 978-1-897039-48-9

www.hip-books.com/fantasy

A teacher's guide is available to cover all three novels.